D0524895

This book belongs to

Josie

Published in 2020 by Alligator Products Ltd.
Cupcake is an imprint of Alligator Products Ltd
2nd Floor, 314 Regents Park Road, London N3 2JX
www.alligatorbooks.co.uk

Copyright © 2020 Alligator Products Ltd

Written by Katherine Sully
Illustrated by Frank Endersby

All rights reserved.
No part of this publication may be reproduced or distributed in any form
or by any means without the permission of the copyright owner.

Printed in China.1623

Hen's Feathers

cupcake

Hetta and Hilda were sisters, but not from the same clutch of eggs. Hetta was older than Hilda.

Hilda had plump, shiny black feathers, sunshine yellow legs and beak, and a beautiful red comb.

Hetta was dull and brown. But she was very kind and took good care of Hilda.

Every morning, long after the cock had crowed, the hens all waddled out of the henhouse looking for their breakfast.

Hilda was very popular with the other hens. She was always in the middle of the crowd, clucking about this and that.

On this particular morning, there was a new hen in the yard. She had fluffy, white feathers. Soon, everyone crowded around to meet her.

The new hen's name was Chantelle. Everyone cooed and clucked, "What a pretty name!" What's more, Chantelle had won a prize at the farm show. Everyone wanted to be her friend.

Except Hilda. Hilda sulked.

"Chantelle's prettier than me," grumbled Hilda. "And she's more popular!"

"Don't be silly, Hilda," said Hetta. "You're just as pretty as Chantelle, but in a different way."

The next morning, Hetta couldn't find Hilda anywhere. Then she spotted the other hens all crowded around Chantelle. She went over to see if Hetta was there.

"You'll never guess what," Chantelle was saying, "...the fox is back!"

There was no sign of Hilda. Now Hetta was really worried – Hilda could be in big trouble if the fox was back!

Hetta rushed all around the farmyard looking for Hilda.

"Have you seen Hilda?" she asked the pig. But he was too busy eating to reply.

"Have you seen Hilda?" she asked the farm cat. But she was too rude to even reply.

"Have you seen Hilda?" she asked the cockerel.

"She was around earlier," he crowed, "disturbing me while I was preening my feathers!"

Hetta went back to the farmyard just in time to see Hilda. She had cockerel feathers stuck to her head and tail and was strutting around the hen coop.

The other hens were giggling behind their wings. Even Hetta had to admit that Hilda looked silly!

That night in the henhouse, Hilda was very cross.

"I don't know why everyone thinks Chantelle's so wonderful," she snapped.

Hetta looked at her sister. "Chantelle is a very nice hen, Hilda," said Hetta.

"Just because her feathers are perfect!" grumbled Hilda.

The following morning, the hens were all in a flutter. During the night, the fox had been back and eggs were missing! The hens gathered outside the henhouse. Hetta looked around. Hilda was missing too!

"Look, over here!" called Chantelle. She had spotted cockerel feathers near a hole in the fence. They crowded around gasping and tutting. It was clear to everyone – the fox had taken Hilda.

The hens did their best to comfort Hetta.

"She was a lovely hen," they clucked. "The best sister you could have wished for."

Hetta was heartbroken!

Just then, Hilda turned up – wearing peacock feathers. She looked ridiculous! But this time, no one was laughing – they were too cross!

That night in the henhouse, Hilda was very upset.

"I just wanted everyone to notice me!" she hiccupped.

"You don't need all these peacock feathers, Hilda," Hetta clucked gently.
"We all love you just as you are..."

Suddenly, they heard a scuffling and a squawking…

Hetta and Hilda rushed out of the henhouse to find the fox with Chantelle...
...IN HIS MOUTH!

As quick as a flash, Hilda plucked a long peacock feather from her tail and tickled the fox's nose.

The fox froze. His nose twitched, his eyes squeezed shut and...
...ATCHOO!

Chantelle shot from this mouth and escaped.

The next morning, the hens gathered to hear about the night's events. Hetta smiled to herself as she spotted Hilda. In the middle of the crowd was her sister with her wing around Chantelle.

"...and that's the best use for a peacock feather I know," chuckled Hilda as she told the story to her crowd of admirers one more time.

The End